AF290806

Life of the Party

Gordon Carrega

Life of the Party
© 2012 by Gordon Carrega (carrega@gmx.de)
Wrong Shoes, Wind Chimes, and Curtains
previously published in The Prose Poem Project
Photos by Ursula Schorn. Book Design by Petra Reisdorf
Published by Books on Demand GmbH, Norderstedt
Printed in Germany
ISBN: 9783848213283

CONTENTS

Gordon Carrega lives in Berlin, Germany, where he works as a freelance English teacher. He has published two previous collections of prose poems, **Back Gate** and **A Place to Stay**.

TODAY

Today's cloaked around me, giving me form. If the day fell away from around me, I'd become invisible. It's a secret relationship, just between me and the day, like we're old friends already, hitting it off with a silent understanding, though we've only just met. The day's not saying anything, just holding me together, carrying me along, and I'm wondering if I should raise questions about yesterday. Could it possibly have been like this yesterday also if I had been somehow different, more aware? But thinking about it makes me dizzy because the question keeps going on all by itself into the past, like a freight train, boxcars rattling, "And the day before? And the day before that? And the day before that?" So I just shut up. I've got promises to keep and I'm moving along, supported, happy for now with the shape I've been given.

MY MAN FRIDAY

Me and my Man Friday, it's not like, "I'll be going out this evening, so have my evening clothes ready by such and such a time." Sure, he's supposed to be doing the chores around here for his room and board, and occasionally he does look like he intends to pick up the duster, get out the broom, make a shopping list, but really I don't like having the dust stirred up, and I'm all for managing on what we already have. Once, I made a list of all that's necessary for a well-stocked pantry, and after creating the long list, I handed it to my Man Friday, saying, "Be sure you buy nothing on this list." We had a good laugh, the laughter going on and on, even days later we couldn't stop bursting into hysterics, repeating the punch-line every time our eyes met. Now I wake up, yawn loudly, roll around in bed, asking myself, would I enjoy having him bring in my morning tea? I crawl out of bed and find him reclining on the couch. "Don't get up, my dear fellow. I can handle things" I make my tea and take my place in the easy chair, exclaiming, "The joys of another languorous day on planet earth! My Man Friday, how well I remember our first encounter." I repeat once more the story of my aloneness, all washed up, doomed to spend the rest of my life without companionship, and one day, the footprints! "Yes, your footprints," I say, observing the look of pride on his impressionable features while I re-enact my redemption, my voice quaking with emotion, "My God! Footprints! Another living soul nearby. I am saved." Falling to my knees, touching the existing footprints on the dusty floor ever so gently with my fingers, tears of joy flowing freely. "Those footprints which I, enraptured by hope, followed to find you, my dear fellow, so similar to these before us now. The rest, as they say, is history," I utter tenderly, taking my seat once again, regaining my composure, noticing that my Man Friday hasn't had his morning nourishment as yet, and I will soon remedy that, serving him a hot cup of tea.

UNBORN SON

A feeling of someone present disturbs my afternoon reverie on the front porch and standing there before me a hazy figure, the ghost of my unborn son. "Pull up a chair," I say, for I had known this reckoning would come one day. The wind is picking up, blurring my vision, and he's fading in and out but at least he's here. Then on my lap a photo album, falling from out of nowhere, an album of all he's missed out on, the pages flipping slowly, allowing me a glimpse of what would have been the usual photos through the years, childhood, adolescence, adulthood, my son maturing, looking more and more like me, the father, and I'm glad to know that it isn't the fate of the unborn to drift through time without any particular experiences to hang on to. I take hold of the album but, up close, these photos, there's just me. Just me in scenarios I know as birth, birthdays, winning prizes, graduation, his wedding, his making something of his life, the usual stuff but no one else in the places where obviously there should be others, no one else, just outlines, not even my son. "Ok, I get the point," I say to the fuzzy vision of my unborn son. "Now you can ask me whatever you want to know. Let's have it out once and for all." His image comes in strongly one moment and, though all sense of age is remarkably absent, he's an adult and I can see the resemblance. Thinking of a memento or two that ought to be handed down, a story or two that ought to outlive me, I get up to allow my unborn son to know at least once in his non-life the embrace from the man who would have been his father. A big wind comes up, the wind tugging at the album in my grasp. My son's gone, just a glimpse of him hovering above the treetops, though he does seem to be looking at me more directly now that he's at a safe distance, the way it tends to be with one's offspring, and a more powerful gust of wind takes the album, takes my son, who is ascending now, and he surely has an entourage of other glimmering unborn souls around him, all those people I couldn't get a glimpse of in the photos, the family and friends from the life he never had.

SKY

I used to go about staring at the clouds, learning names of cloud formations. Then a new interest developed, walking about in the moonlight, wanting to discover something particular about the moonlight. Soon after, seeing the stars in the daytime became my objective, and one day I started savoring the different heavenly hues, but my interest in colors faded away and now it's just the sky. Colors don't matter anymore, clouds don't matter, neither the stars nor the moon, sunny days don't matter, and after looking up at the sky, letting time go by while I repeat to myself sky, sky, sky, after that I go walking about, looking like someone who's been asking for help for so long that his pleas have lost all sense of urgency.

SELF-PORTRAIT WITH DEATH Arnold Böcklin 1827–1901

Is this painting important to me or am I making it so because I want to write
something and weeks ago I wrote in my notebook "Self-portrait with Death",
a reminder to write about going up to the museum, sitting on the nearby bench,
Mr. Death in skeletal form, his macabre jaws gleefully parted, hollow eye sockets
knowing what's he got a right to. He's perched just over the artist's shoulder, playing his fiddle in the artist's ear, the artist in the painting, paint brush poised in one
hand, suspended movement, palette in the other hand, his head tilted slightly
back, listening, not turning to look, his heedful eyes, like questions fixed on me,
focuses out from the canvas while death fiddles on. The leisure of a free afternoon, I head on up to the museum, the portrait of the artist, distracted from his
work by the melody of death's fiddle, the two of us listening together.

SHADOW

Still have my shadow on your wall as a memento or has it fallen into obscurity? Obscurity, more shadowy, is preferable to neglect. My shadow is a memento of regret when I remember the last time my shadow passed over your sleep. This incessant casting of shadow works both ways, me and my shadow, we have each other, and my shadow will accompany me to my grave. I don't spend enough time communing with my shadow, nor am I very often on the lookout for my shadow, nor do I think too much about whether my shadow will enjoy the party, and I do have a favorite stroll but I have not engaged my shadow in the discussion of pros and cons. From the absolute elsewhere where I've never been, my shadow has come to be with me. Once I spoke to my shadow. "Be strong," I said. "I can only bring forth what is within me," my shadow whispered to its shadowy friends. My shadow is not as restless as me. My shadow would be equally satisfied to live a life without events. "Remember! The firing squad stood absolutely still but their shadows were seen to quiver." An age-old warning usually said to someone about to undertake a shady task. First the word remember is spoken, then a pause of several seconds during which the speaker waves both hands wildly in front of the face of the listener's shadow. "Whoever you are, could you please get your shadow the hell out of here," shouted by a woman while sunbathing, without even opening her eyes, my shadow passing over her recumbent form. My shadow looks a whole lot better in that hat than I do.

SUNSET

Experts on sunset watching enjoy participating in this activity either alone or with others of equal caliber. You've never learned to watch a sunset? No, but I can watch a silhouette. Please take me by the hand and teach me the art of sunset watching. Let's practice some more with imagined sunsets in the privacy of my room. No, but I can watch a black candle with a black flame. A sunset is reasonably complete in itself except for the service of memory. You're doing it wrong. You don't see what I see. You're too anxious, like the sunset is a horse or something. Seems to me that you're trying to eat your sunset and have it too. Surely this sunset has happened before for eternity is fresh out of what's original. If you're standing up you don't have a lap but if you sit right down next to me I can put my head in your lap and wait for the sun to set.

GREY

No overarching heavens today, just low ceiling of grey, flat, implacable clouds, no grey masses rolling about with glimmer of light lurking in the lining, no ominous darkening drifting in from any direction, but a levelled greyness, and me, huddling into myself, not looking at the pedestrians striding by, my eyes following the sidewalk's narrative, then stopping, everyone detouring around me while I take my stance, hands shoved into coat pockets, body arching slightly back, looking up long and hard at the absolute two-dimensional bleakness from which no angels will venture out, no dreamy visions, no bright songs. Waiting to cross the street, leaning against a lamppost, enough sun coming out at the perfect angle to cast my shadow directly on the square patch of sunlit pavement in front of me like a black and white photo negative, shadow of a man leaning against shadow of a lamp post.

SAM

This guy comes up to me at a party, "Sam, is it really you? Sam, it's been a long time." Wonderful seeing his dear friend Sam again, all choked up with tears of joy, only problem, I'm not Sam. A bear hug, patting me on the back, my voice trying to communicate I'm not Sam getting muffled against his shoulder, rapid fire excerpts about the great old days with good buddy Sam, laughing uproariously one moment, crying with nostalgic pleasure the next, a knee slapping routine, "Remember Sam, remember our knee-slapping? Come on Sam, for old time's sake." And I do get influenced, under the spell of comradeship, drawn into this ritual, managing a brief flurry before regaining my composure, not wanting to create false hopes. The party coming to a standstill around us, the gaping happy faces witnessing this encounter of dear old friends, me saying, "I'm not Sam. I'm really not Sam," turning to the other guests for validation, hoping for someone to step forward, interceding on my behalf, saying, "I know this guy and I can assure you he's not Sam." I'm also a bit regretful at not being Sam, wanting to say, yes I remember, I remember all that you're saying, all the good times, but I can only honestly utter, "Sorry, I'm not Sam. That knee-slapping was just a bit of fun but indeed I'm not Sam." He's saying, "Sam I've always wanted to tell you how sorry I am that I never..." leaning in close, whispering an elliptical apology that I can't really get because of course I don't know the background, and help finally does appear, a perceptive woman, picking up on my perplexity, raises the question, "When did you last see your friend Sam?" The guy answering matter-of-factly, "At his funeral four years ago." A hush falls over the proceedings. "Your friend Sam is dead?" the woman asks in a resonant, friendly, reasonable manner, the man, releasing me, turning to his audience, "Yes my old friend Sam is dead but when I saw this guy here," he says, putting his arm around my shoulder, "I thought he does look a bit like Sam, just enough, so I figured I'll pour my heart out to him like he was Sam. Now I want to thank you for the few precious minutes of being Sam." We're shaking hands, him asking, "Do I remind you of someone? Someone you haven't seen in a long time, someone maybe who's dead, dead or alive, someone you might want to say a few words to?" I'm staring at him, his face drifting into memory, more and more familiar, who does he remind me of?

HOPES

Death will come and find me right in this very dwelling, and my ghost will remain, the person moving in, most likely someone much the same as I'd been back then, when I took up residence here. Glad to find a place he could afford, settling down with a few scattered objects of old furniture. I'll be here, shade of my former self, keeping a merciful eye on his misfortunes, no way to help in any case, his wrong decisions piling up, the next desperate phone call. Days of not getting out the door, all dressed he sits down, a man waiting for a taxi he knows in advance will never come. Ghosts are not forever, the final curtain some day and I'm all gone, meanwhile taking in the old familiar one-man drama, nodding sagely now while the scenes unfold like clouds before my eyes, his talking to the walls, rehearsing reasons to explain his languishing, weighing each reason to decide whether it's a good reason or a bad reason or really just an excuse masquerading as a reason. Waiting for a knock at the door but not caring if it will ever happen, exploring the difference between being a man who should have done something with his life but didn't, or a man who simply didn't. Even if the phantom taxi were to arrive, where would he ask to be taken? Saying, in a voice hazy with philo-sophical pleasure, "I'm the man who didn't."

WASTE

This particular day is passing and I'm not waiting for anything. I can imagine someone asking "What are you waiting for?" Kind of like a challenge, or to mock me because I'm doing nothing that suggests getting on with my life. I'm just hanging around, so I can understand that I'm giving the impression of waiting. I can hear the words, "You're wasting your life," as if spoken by an authority from above, which causes me to chuckle, to reply quietly to myself, "I have placed my faith in wasting my life so actually I'm following my chosen path." I've never really said these words out loud to anybody because there's nobody I trust enough not to taunt me later, when things get really bad, saying, "Well you did say that you have placed your faith in wasting your life, so what now?" But I like saying those words to myself because it sounds like I'm a man who has taken a strong stand on an important issue. It's as if I'm rehearsing, getting ready for the day I'll be called upon to give a significant speech. "Waste what you have. Place your faith in waste," I say, standing in front of the mirror, getting a little melancholy, wondering to whom would I possibly give such advice?

TICKETS

I've got a hot date coming up and a friend accompanies me to pick up the theatre tickets in advance, choosing the best seats in the house. I turn away from the counter, slipping the tickets into my shirt pocket, the friend putting his hands to his eyes, pretending to be holding a camera, saying, "The man about town preparing for new romance! Hold that pose." He knows a cocktail bar nearby, the perfect location for an intimate after-theatre drink, and we go by to check it out, drinking a toast to the best of what is yet to come, my friend, once again pretending to be snapping a photo, saying, "You've got that Casanova look. Hold that pose." At home, I stick the tickets in the frame of the mirror where I always take a look at myself before leaving my apartment, the tickets so officially promising, and when the friend drops by a few days later, glancing at himself in the mirror and noticing the tickets, I have to explain that the woman broke the date, how I spent the disheartening evening alone at home, drowning my sorrows, imagining the two empty seats in the centre of the otherwise full house, a summing up of my great expectations. He says I should definitely not leave the unused, outdated tickets stuck in the frame of the mirror, for doing so will be much worse than a black cat crossing my path, or the seven years bad luck from breaking a mirror. I say leave me with my souvenir of what never came to pass, but he dashes for the tickets, setting them ablaze in the ashtray, adding the theatre program lying on the table, so I have to take the flaming ashtray and step out onto the balcony, letting the wind take the smoke. I'm about to re-enter the living room, let my friend have a does of my anger, and he raises his imaginary camera, "The bon vivant standing in the doorway to his balcony. Hold that pose!"

NO ONE

No one listens to me. I'm not excluded, nor am I actually ignored, but no one cares about what I say. They will have me come along but then what? "Wait a minute," I say and they all stop and wait. I say, "Let's turn here." Sure fine, they all agree, "You seem to know where you're going." We turn here but I don't know where we're going, and even when we're completely lost, do they remember it's my fault? They simply babble along, turning here and there until we manage to get back on some kind of track, and all I'm left with is the feeling of how indifferent they all are to what I do or don't do. I say, "You have no idea what I'm going through." Another of the gang dominates the conversation, saying, "Tell us, man, blurt it out. Are you going through hell, man? Is that it, a season in hell?" "I suppose you're right," I agree. "It's all a bit hellish." But it's like my words are dribbling away because there isn't a particular list of questions that I want to be asked, and my thoughts are just a vague and meandering inquiry into the meaning of it all, so how can I begin to formulate anything real with them staring at me, waiting for a series of facts to hang on to? "You've got us, old boy. You're not alone, you know." "I certainly feel alone." That's what I feel but of course I don't speak those words. We all share a hearty embrace and then it's business as usual, a blurring of opinions about one thing or another, everyone laughing to beat the band. But I'm not laughing. Does anyone ask why I'm not laughing? Or are they just too taken up by their own laughter even to notice? Or upon noticing just say to themselves, "So he's not laughing! Must I give a damn? I am laughing. He doesn't have to laugh if he doesn't want to." I cling to my dearest and nearest, though even her attitude is hard to understand. "Don't you think you're exaggerating? Everyone really cares about you." But I can see that she's distracted by her own uncertainty, even when she embraces me, saying, "Come darling, lets hold each other and together we'll make it through another long night."

A GOOD TALK

Out and about, striding along, staring up at the clouds, staring down at the grey sidewalk, bemoaning the efforts in my life that have all come to naught, I am greeted by a middle-aged successful-looking fellow who greets me by name, asking in a voice brimming with sincerity, "How are you doing today?" "Fine, just fine," I answer, having no interest in interrupting the mental reviewing of the failures I have accrued so far in my lifetime, not even bothering to ask how come he knows my name, and it happens again, this time a young man and woman, college students one would assume from their appearance, who, with concern in their voices, call out my name along with a cheerful greeting, stopping directly in front of me, forcing me to walk around them in order to continue on my way. The same scenario keeps reoccurring throughout my aimless meanderings, the calling out of my name by persons unbeknownst to me, the question "How are you doing today," the questioner prepared to stand and talk, for example a woman bearing a startling resemblance to my mother who gives me the kind of maternally sustaining stare that could easily lead all the way back to my room in the attic, a man wearing a beret and carrying an easel, about to set up on a corner to do some painting, and he apparently wants to get me standing still long enough to pry my secrets out of me, a police officer stationed at a busy intersection, which of course causes me more than a flutter of anxiety, huddling into my identity, increasing my pace, and other assorted run-of-the-mill characters one comes across in an aimless afternoon stroll through the city, all wanting to know how I' doing, how I'm getting on. And when an attractive woman takes her turn, it seems the right time to ask "What's going on here? What's the occasion?" "We care about you, caring about you is the occasion," she answers with deeply felt sisterly solicitude. I'm about to insist on my right to privacy but her tearful eyes melt my resolve, and I notice that all the good folks who have so far accosted me have been tagging along, hovering at a discrete distance. "Let's all gather by the river and have a good talk about you, our main concern," the woman demands, signalling the others, taking hold of my arm, she and I leading the way.

ON BONGOLAI

I've got my hut by the river here on Bongolai, all the papaya, plantain, and mango trees I need. I'm at one with the natural forces, watching the sunrise, watching the sunset, lulling about by the Bongolai River, swimming, romping with the monkeys that come out of the trees to dance with me, the distant roaring of a lonely lion or laughter of a hyena providing nightly accompaniment to my dreams. One afternoon, just as I've begun another painting of the sunlight on the water, a woman who has been having an afternoon swim emerges from the river. I had assumed that no human other than I lived on Bongolai, and, striking up a conversation, I ask for her opinion on my art work, telling her that I would love to show her my other watercolors back at the hut. But art is not her interest, her story tumbling out about her husband who wants to leave Bongolai and she wants to stay and he keeps leaving and coming back, leaving and coming back, unable to stick to a decision, this back and forth going on already for several weeks. "I just can't stand it anymore," she shrieks, her cry, carried along through the trees, causing the scampering away of all life-forms within hearing distance, silencing the scintillating sounds of nature, except for the steady murmur of the river on the rocks, the hush of the breeze through the boughs, a distant trumpeting of an elephant. I ask why would anybody ever want to leave Bongolai and that's exactly how she feels, but her husband has discovered that lying about all day, entranced by the wild beauty, does not provide enough sense of purpose. He's languishing, so he wants to go back to the mainland and resume his business career. I allow her to persuade me to accompany her back to the conjugal hut, to witness the scene of her misery, and we stand, well-protected from human eyes, beneath the boughs of a banyan tree, observing her husband who, dressed in a tie and pin-striped business suit, waits in the clearing, frantically bellowing out her name, startling a flock of flamingos nesting nearby. "His knowing there's another man in the picture will only complicate matters," she says. "Goodbye for now. I must go to him." She steps up to her husband who, in a harsh decisive tone, proclaims, "This time I'm going for sure." Holding onto his briefcase, he walks hastily away, a man marching off to catch a commuter train. I scurry up a mangrove tree, reaching the top with great exertion, a lookout point that allows me to observe the retreating husband making his determined way toward the sandbar where he will be able to go across to the mainland. Arriving at the crossing, he halts, turning around, tormented by indecision, crying out beseechingly the name of his dear wife, jumping up and down, running this way and that, frenzied and anguished, his screams vibrating in the stillness as he races back from whence he came, hurtling madly through the dense undergrowth. "He's returning," I inform the wife from my position high in the tree. She howls in distress, "He's driving me crazy." With determination, she adds, "But stand by him I will." The lost deranged soul comes careening back, dropping his briefcase at his wife's feet, tearing off his tie and jacket, rushing into his wife's ambivalent embrace. "I'll never leave you, never!" he exclaims. Arm in arm they make their way into the humble hut and, unnoticed, I scamper down from the tree and go lie on the riverbank, staring up at the sky, enjoying the cloud formations. The next afternoon, while sitting by the river with my sketch book, trying to capture the soaring of an eagle, the woman, a lei of lilies around her neck, once again distracts my attention. "Now I must be getting back for my husband needs me," she says, after taking an appropriate interest in my sketch of the eagle. She asks, "Will you walk with me again as you did just yesterday?" Sheltered from view by the overhanging boughs, we once again observe the torment of her husband who's ready to depart for a day at the office. "Goodbye, I must go to him," she says, his wretched cries filling the afternoon air, the situation of the previous day repeating itself, except that I manage with greater ease the climb to my lookout point, a perch from which I observe the husband's agonizing departure and return, circumstances having conspired to grant an added attraction to my days on Bongolai.

BRAWN

We're expecting dinner guests. Jan's taking care of some last minute details in the kitchen. I'm strolling about the living room in my freshly washed, close-fitting black jeans and brand new white silk shirt, taller than usual in my brightly polished ankle-high boots, then the noise of something falling and Jan's calling out for me to give her a hand, a shelf in the fridge having come undone. No disaster, not much has splashed to the floor, just a matter of removing some items, setting the shelf right, cleaning up the slight mess. Jan suggests that I take off my shirt and she assists me with the unbuttoning, assists with the graceful shedding of the shirt by standing behind me, peeling away the soft material from my shoulders, my arms slipping out of the long sleeves. Jan hangs the shirt on the back of a chair and I'm shirtless in the kitchen, fussing with the matter at hand, feeling sleek in my tight jeans and snazzy boots, enjoying the pleasure of the domestic air on my bare skin, taking my time to be efficient. "Thank you dear," Jan says, touching me on my naked chest, stroking her fingers along my biceps. She's moving about, getting things in order for our dinner party, her casual touch on my exposed chest and arms, a most natural gesture of appreciation for my assistance, but she also wants to move me aside because I'm in her way, standing in the middle of the kitchen with my shirt off, keenly self-conscious of being a man standing in the kitchen with his shirt off, his fashionable white shirt hanging decently on the back of a kitchen chair. Not in itself an unusual situation but I'm feeling misplaced, something about Jan's touch on my naked chest, and maybe because I had been already properly attired for our dinner party and then my shirt readily removed, demonstrating my willingness to take the necessary action, stripping down, and maybe because Jan's all stylishly dressed up and I'm also decked out in my favorite boots and tight jeans, without a shirt. Now it would be a simple matter to put my shirt on again but precisely because I'm a man with his shirt off in the kitchen while his wife is preoccupied with getting everything in order for the invited friends, so busy with her duties that she can touch her husband indifferently on his unclothed chest, and stroke her fingers along his biceps, saying in a most natural voice, "Thank you dear", all being the most commonplace of occurrences and for the very reason that it is so ordinary, it seems also most run-of-the-mill to remain shirtless, strolling about with my hands in my pockets, savoring on my uncovered chest the enticing mix of cool air from the open living room window and the cozy temperature, along with the appetizing fragrances, emanating from the kitchen, my leather heels sounding out my contemplative footsteps. Pausing in front of the mirror to observe my physique, wondering quietly to myself how much swagger is appropriate while moving about in my own home with my shirt off, my wife bustling about, pretty much ignoring me, until she says, "Shouldn't you be getting your shirt on?"

UNREQUITED

"Unrequited love," she says, her lips forming the phrase with didactic care, her tongue delicately caressing each syllable, the two of us together like it's just another normal afternoon, having a cup of tea at my place, following my weeks of crazed and sleepless nights, frenzied letters, ringing her up at all hours, finally her agreeing to come by, to offer whatever explanations she can to help ease my torment. She's consoling me, talking about unrequited love and I must accept that there's now someone else in her life. Glancing away from her, I catch sight of my face in the mirror on the wall, noticing how strangely gaunt I've become, unshaven and unkempt, my blazing eyes like someone biblical, too desperate these past weeks to think much about bodily sustenance, the phrase unrequited love opening new vistas in my brain. "Unrequited love," I repeat with even more thoughtful enunciation, and her eyes radiate compassion while she says that by my contemplating the full experience of unrequited love I will move my suffering out of the mundane realm of heartbreak, transform my agony of rejection, thereby achieving another more transcendent dimension. In my feverish condition, her every utterance contains divine wisdom, and waves of exhilaration flow over me, for I'm ready to accept all her teachings, her instructions taking me to the very threshold of my mission in life, the one who has been lost in the wilderness of unrequited love, who has explored the heart of darkness contained therein, and has returned, transformed, to hold forth on its true essence. I chant quietly to myself the phrase 'unrequited love', rapture filling my enlightened heart. She says I seem suddenly blissful, almost saintly, and I smile beatifically, for I'm already considering where the altar should be placed, which photo of her will be enlarged and framed to serve as the center piece, certainly flowers will be needed, incense, candles and an elegant candleholder, sacred objects, such as the occasional notes she sent my way, that silk scarf she gave me for my birthday, the lipstick-stained cup she's now drinking out of will go directly on the holy table, and, noticing the piece of colorful costume jewellery she's wearing, I say, "Would you mind letting me have that brooch as a keepsake?"

MY VOICE

I don't have a well-modulated voice with resonant timbre but my voice has a willingness to register surprise, sorrow, joy, puzzlement, or whatever's called for at the moment of conversing, a way of being in tune with the subject under consideration, and my voice can become high-pitched, even shrill, or soft, barely a whisper one moment, only to explode the next, to howl, to guffaw, to become mellow, intimate, thoughtful, ponderous even, but at the precise moment. My voice can utter a simple phrase, like "How are things?" in a perfect tone of intimacy and concern so that depths of communicative possibilities open up, or my voice can express "Right, that's right. I really know what you mean, for we all must have some kind of life", or any of a hundred other similar heartening words in such a manner that you feel inspired to go on talking, delving into yourself, exploring your need for language, and my voice knows how to skilfully insert into the dialogue an anecdote or two that strike the required note, harmonizing with what you want to impart, thereby fuelling the impulse for discourse. Of course it's not only my voice but also the accompanying body language, head thrown back in laughter, or lowered in commiseration, or a frown while I lean forward, my hand stroking my chin, my shoulders hunched, or suddenly sitting bolt upright, eyes bright with amazement. My voice reflects back the revelation in what has been said, adding, when appropriate, a decorative frill, or depth and resonance, or turning a simple, straightforward remark from a potential conversation partner, for example, "I thought there would be more people at the party," or "I just can't stand getting up in the morning, not one more morning" into a gem of observation to be examined for philosophical implications, and doing this with the most unassuming air, slight apparently random comments arising unaffectedly on the spur of the moment, perhaps put forward first with gentle laughter, leading to mild philosophical intensity, my head nodding, upper body inclining in a gesture of brotherhood, inviting a compassionate tête à tête, thereby inciting you to enquire further, questioning your own assumptions, and to know you're not alone in some incomprehensible, banal suffering, and when I'm all talked out, standing off to the side, listening to the voices carrying on without mine, echoes of my own voice in the voices of others.

AT FIRST SIGHT

Another grim morning on the bus, squeezed into the standing room only crowd, assailed by dour faces and quiet desperation, the bus of our fate making its regular stops, passengers getting on, and I'm standing face to face with a woman who has just boarded, shoved up close to her, barely avoiding full body contact, and the warmth of romance flooding through me assures me right off that she's the woman I've been waiting and hoping for all the mornings of my life. Her face agape with the joy of love, the depths of her eyes opening ever deeper to allow me entry, offer clear evidence that she knows we are meant for each other, knows that years from now we'll be reminiscing about this moment, recalling for our friends how me met one morning on the bus, hemmed in together on our way to work, thrown together for eternity. We're lost in each other, disappearing together with each swooning breath into our shared visions of Sundays all day in bed, whispering sweet nothings, laughing together on Saturday nights at the movies, holidays chasing each other along the tropical beach, candlelit dinners in fancy restaurants, a state of wonder, a joyous speechlessness, our auras blending into one expansive radiance, for we just have to stand facing each other and this miracle will continue, the other passengers becoming aware of this blessed occurrence, the love emanating from us, the atmosphere on the bus lightening up, the previously grim faces now beaming with joy, their glowing eyes upon us filled with best wishes, and though we're all just as packed in as ever, the bus making it's monotonous journey in the heavy traffic, all the worries about being late for work evaporate, the newspapers held by the passengers lowered to afford them the holy sight of true love which the woman and I embody. The driver gives a beep of his horn and other horns beep loudly. a joyful beeping, my beloved and I swooning together. Then the bus lurches and my dearest is falling, falling away from me. I should reach out, take hold of her, stop her fall, and she's expecting me to do just that, my every sense telling me to act, save the woman I love from falling. But I'm paralyzed and she falls, her face going pale with the shock of my doing nothing to help. No danger really for there's hardly room to really fall but enough room to fall away from me, to fall, for example as she does, across the laps of two seated passengers whose eyes, directed at me, overflow with fire and brimstone condemnation. I want to say, "Although we're experiencing this miracle of love I don't know you and I can't just reach out and take hold of you just like that." Assisted by other passengers, she has already righted herself, standing on her own two feet, and her seething distress is palpable, not only hers but everyone else, incensed at my not having done the manly thing, the quiet desperation even worse now because scorn has been added, scorn directed at me, newspapers snapping open once again, the dismayed spectators huddling into themselves, all, once again, distress and dashed hopes.

GHOST STORY

Sitting around with my circle of friends, candlelight dinner, fireplace aflame with hospitality, conversations veering off in all directions, charming wit and uproarious laughter. Sipping from my wine goblet, I drift away, lost in reverie, the faces of my dearest and nearest friends taking on a beatific radiance, a timeless resonance to every word, scintillating echoes down the boulevards of memory. A ghostly voice whispers in my ear, "Sorry to intrude but this is your ghost speaking, taking the opportunity to get some advance instructions while you're still in the land of the living, just wondering if these are some of the nice folks you'll be wanting me to call on once you're among the dearly departed?" I glance discreetly over my shoulder but what do I expect? Of course my ghost is nowhere to be seen for I'm still here in the flesh. Experiencing an exquisite thrill of comradeship and kindness for this invisible visitor from the great beyond who's gracious enough to consult me on such an important matter, I offer my best social smile to signal my ongoing delight with the evening, a good camouflage while I commune silently and leisurely with my ghost, saying, yes, nostalgia and commemoration would be well-served if, when I'm no longer among the living, my friends were to be visited by him, my faithful shade. Especially at a time like this when they're all gathered together, if he would, with just enough visibility to be detected, hopefully more than on one occasion, simply float through the atmosphere. My ghost suggests that I go over by the fireplace, that I focus on the scene as if I were taking a group photo, for this will serve to impress upon him the visual data which will be helpful at a later date, and I find myself, under his control, rising effortlessly like a cloud, levitating across the room, set down in front of the fireplace, a location that allows the perfect angle for a group photo, including my empty chair, and there's a camera-like click in my brain before I'm wafted back into my seat, reaching again for my goblet, settling into the sparkling mystery of my existence and the joy of good friends, my ghost, thanking me for my willingness to cooperate, drifting off, leaving me to face alone the gaping faces of my dear friends, bewildered eyes fixed on me. "Did you see that? Did you see him float off and come back? I know I saw it. We all saw it. My God, who is this man we call our friend?"

CLASSICAL

I'm sitting on the bench at the bus stop when I hear the hard, well-paced strides of a woman in high heels, a tall brunette, classically beautiful, wearing red high heels, a short, low-cut, sleeveless, tight-fitting black dress, a small, black patent-leather shoulder bag bouncing to the rhythm of her slender hips, bracelets jangling on her swinging arms. Her hair, tied severely back, shows off her stark, gaunt features, and full, startlingly bright red lips. She's pale, a vibrant paleness, even more emphasized in the sunshine and in contrast with the flimsy black dress, and I can't imagine she'd ever not be pale. She heads directly at me, apparently intent on addressing me, some information about the bus schedule perhaps. I sit up straight, smiling charmingly, but her eyes, her green eyes, are pure fury. She's coming closer, the space between us shimmering with fury, all hers, the phrase, "A terrible beauty," flashes in my mind as I utter a timid, hopeful, "Good morning." My voice catches her by surprise. Had she been oblivious to my presence just wanting to have a seat next to me? She turns in her determined stride, moves away, and begins to pace, with measured intensity, back and forth. She leans against the lamppost, impatiently tapping one foot on the sidewalk. Every morning just she and I at the bus stop and she's always chic, always a similar version of black dress, and always as if something has just occurred to make her aflame with contained rage. I tell myself I'll simply ignore her but my ears are attuned to the rhythm of her footsteps and once again she catches my eyes, transfixed by her fiery stare. It's as if she's expecting something from me, calling out to me, while daring me to continue looking at her one moment longer, and at the same time I can't be sure that her stare isn't accidental, impersonal, perhaps not even focused on me but just in my direction. A forlorn, "Good morning," dutifully escapes me. She turns away. I can hear her breathing, the rhythmic tapping of her shoe on the pavement. Our bus is always full. She enters first. so it's impossible to avoid standing close behind her, her breathing still charged. She gets off a few stops before mine and after she exits I feel slightly dizzy, wanting to laugh merrily, to make small talk with anyone. A morning comes and she doesn't appear, morning after morning passing without her. I'm haunted by a bewildering feeling of having somehow let her down, and one afternoon during my lunch hour I catch sight of a woman, same classical beauty, same hair style, black dress, same stride, surely the woman from the bus stop. She enters a department store and keeping a discreet distance, I follow her, tenderness rising up in my heart at having the opportunity to see her again. Advancing through the store, stopping at the lingerie department, she takes an interest in the various styles of intimate apparel, a black negligee holding her attention. She walks on and I'm right behind, lurking about, getting ready to approach her. She's now in the dress department. I'm on my lunch hour and I can't keep slinking around like I have all the time in the world so finally I stand directly across from her as she removes a black dress from the rack. She's holding the dress against her body, checking the size, and she's just about to turn and look in the mirror when she catches sight of me, staring. Her eyes widen and quiver for a moment, her stare just as glaring, unwavering, as challenging as ever. I will myself to meet her eyes. "We know each other. The bus stop, we know each other from the bus stop." She places the dress over the rack. She moistens her lips. I feel stunned by the very echo of my own voice repeating in my mind the words I had just formulated. Her voice, firm with conviction, "I never take the bus." Striding away in her usual fierce manner, I call out after her, "Anymore, you mean you never take the bus anymore."

LIFE OF THE PARTY

The party is in full swing and I'm standing off to the side near the buffet, picking at the bowl of olives, feeling like a castaway on the tide of laughter and fellowship, when a woman eases up to me and says, "Not much of a social life, no circle of friends, been invited out of mere kindness on the part of our host, is that about right?" "I didn't know it showed," I manage to reply. "You need to make your presence felt," she advises, adding, "for no man is an island." I share with her my secret longing to, at least once in my waking life, find myself up at the lake for the weekend, and come Monday morning I'll be able to say 'I was up at the lake this weekend with my circle of friends, horseback riding, swimming, sailing, playing tennis. What a time I had with that old gang of mine.'" "You mean you've never experienced the splendour of such an utterance!" she exclaims. Then she asks, "Who would you say is the life of this party?" I indicate a handsome fellow, his convivial, vibrant force going out to everyone, the partygoers swept up in his sheer magnetism and resonant good cheer. She informs me that the life of the party is none other than her husband, and, basking in his glory, she points out certain details of his style, helping me to understand the dynamics of being the life of the party revealed in the display before us, laughter ringing free, gleeful voices rising and falling, the party taking on the radiance of perfection, following a divine script, and right in the middle of his grand cascading of joy and camaraderie, the life of the party stands deadly still, staring at his wife and me, his eyes ablaze with fury, careening toward us, knocking over the revellers blocking his path, coming to a halt in front of his spouse, raising his arms in tormented appeal, gasping for breath, "How can I be the life of the party when you stand here analyzing me, making me unbearably self-conscious? You of all people should know it doesn't come easy for me to be the life of the party and I'm not a freak of nature to be scrutinized and discussed." And his wife, taking him in a motherly embrace, calming him down, whispers in his ear, "Remember dear, you'll be needed up at the lake next weekend."

PARIS AND DIE

"See Paris and die," my father used to say, meaning that seeing Paris would be the fulfillment of his life's desire. "See Paris and die," he would sing out regardless of the music as he got drunk and danced across the floor, hands raised above his head, fingers snapping to his own rhythm. Come morning he always went off in his crisp white shirt to his office job, saying, "Got to get to Paris" to give himself the incentive to go out the door for another day's pay. And he must have sung, "See Paris and die," in the arms of Cherie, his French girlfriend who worked in a perfume store where they met when my father purchased Parisian Nights, a birthday gift for my mother, the fragrance becoming a stale, deadening fixture in the atmosphere of our small flat after my mother hurled the bottle of perfume at him, smashing it against the wall that night he left for good. By the time I got around to visiting my father, so many years had passed that I had already walked the streets of Paris, had been to the top of the Eiffel Tower and proclaimed, "See Paris and Die." With my girlfriend, each of us in a black beret, I had danced on Pont Notre Dame while the musicians earning money on the bridge played "The Last Time I Saw Paris." In a Paris café I'd had a photo taken of my girlfriend and me together, which I sent off in an envelope to my father with a postcard showing Paris by night on which I had written, "See Paris and die." No, he had never gotten to Paris, and perhaps he could say, "Je ne regrette rien," and the whole business with Cherie had been a disaster, her returning to Paris, with the plan that he would join her there, plans that just drifted away like the smoke from her Gauloise cigarettes. Sitting together in his dismal apartment, drinking a bottle of chardonnay, he held up a photo, the photo he had framed of me with my former girlfriend in the Paris cafe. "Still have the same girl?" he asked. My memories floated to the tune of The Last Time I Saw Paris and I said, "No, I no longer have the same girl." "C'est la vie, c'est la vie," he said over and over again until I had no choice but to echo along, the two of us adding in chorus, "See Paris and die, see Paris and die."

WRONG SHOES

No matter how much time I take trying on the shoes, testing them in the store by walking around, looking into those abbreviated shoe mirrors, their up from under view somehow giving me the feeling of being part of the ruling class, no matter how much caution I exercise, a few days after beginning to wear my new shoes the fact becomes tragically clear that I'm once again in the nightmare of having chosen the wrong shoes. My walking becomes a hectic kind of hobbling about, engaged in the impossible dance of attempting not to step on either tortured foot, but step I must, moving along, hopping and shuffling. With my next purchase I choose a pair of sturdy shoes, try them on hurriedly, take a step or two in the store, exclaim, "I'll take them," lay the cash on the counter, run out the store, leaving my old shoes behind gaping penitently at me, and I get in step with the smooth forward motion of the crowd of pedestrians. The days pass, everything fine and dandy regarding my new shoes, then one morning, on my way to catch the bus, I begin to limp, a subtle limping, a graceful limp so unlike the shambling, faltering, staggering motion that had been the result of my previous pairs of new shoes, and the condition remains stable, never more than a subdued limp, along with a facial expression seasoned with world-weariness.

BEAUTIFUL WIFE

Getting out of bed, entering the kitchen to assist my wife with the breakfast, I'm stunned to discover that overnight she's turned into a raving beauty like a wholesomely glamorous Hollywood leading lady in everyday garments. I blurt out, "What in heaven's name's going on here?" At least that's what I intend to utter but, not wanting to sound accusing, I bite my tongue and remain in a state of awe, wondering what new burden of responsibility will be added to my days from this moment on. I exclaim, "You've always been a good-looking woman but suddenly you're a radiant knock-out beauty queen. What on earth has happened to you?" At least that's what I'd like express but I decide instead to appear nonchalant, to whistle a happy tune, go back into the bedroom, intending to hideout for a spell and ponder my destiny, but in no time at all I'm back in the kitchen with her, willing to pretend it's just another ordinary morning, enchanted by the fragrance of coffee. She's standing by the window, her seraphic voice articulating the simple words, "Beautiful sky! What a beautiful sky." I take my dutiful place beside her and focus on the sky. "Look at all the angelic wispy pink clouds," she says, pointing out this attraction with a graceful waving of her hand, and it surely seems to me that's she herself is creating the picturesque clouds and the most breathtaking blue sky for our viewing pleasure because the awesome beauty only becomes visible to my eyes when she indicates its existence. Trying to tune into the occasion by imitating the melody of her voice, I say, "Sure is a beautiful sky this morning." At least that's what I want to say but instead I say nothing and turn away, speechless, staring dumbfounded at the most ordinary objects, the coffee cup that has suddenly appeared in my hand for I am completely unaware of having taken hold of it, and the cup seems an object of great value because it's the cup she drinks out of every morning. Shaking with bewilderment, I accidentally drop the cup, which doesn't shatter on the floor, almost a hoped for sound of banal disaster which might serve to break whatever spell I'm under, but the goddess who is my wife manages with sovereign grace to catch the cup before it hits the floor, and, like it's the most ordinary occurrence, offers a gracious smile and hands the cup back to me. I can't stand this trembling that's come over me caused by us being so close together, almost bumping into each other while we're throwing together our usual breakfast, and the fact of her neither putting on airs nor lording it over me with her beauty makes the situation that much harder. "I'll be right back," I manage to gasp and make a quick exit, placing myself at a location from which I can observe her through the entry to the kitchen, her effortless, opulent gestures, the joy and splendor that she's radiating. She catches me staring and waves at me, a little flutter of her fingers, and all the while I'm reasoning with myself, saying, "Just face it, your normally attractive mate and companion has been transformed, most likely by divine intervention, into a heavenly creature, which is certainly an occasion for praise and gratitude instead of this foolish cowering." Then a flash of light! My celestial companion, having taken hold of her most ordinary camera, has snapped my photo, saying "I just had to get this shot of you with that most amazing look of serenity on your normally somewhat grim face."

HOME AGAIN

The night air, a lush element, luxuriant with shades of myself accumulated from all my goings to and fro on this very same daily street, the dark windows like phantom witnesses listening in on my thoughts, I catch a glimpse of a falling star, too late to make a wish, and staring up at the heavens consider the speed of light and light years and black holes and the dying stars and how it is that the light reaching me here on earth could have been emitted from a star already dead, the light traveling through space and time with nowhere to return to, light without a home, and when I turn into the walkway to my cottage it's all so automatic, the taking out of my keys, selecting the door key, ready to insert the key into the lock, to open the door. But tonight, I move languidly away from the door, letting the key-ring fall back into my pocket, walk around back and when I reach the small patio, sheltered by the dark pine looming above my cottage, I look through the sliding glass door into the darkness that contains my desk, enough light from the dying stars for me to perceive the mug from my morning coffee still resting near an opened book, the towel I had thrown over the back of my chair after showering, my old slippers with the alive look of a sad, faithful pet. I sit down in the rocking-chair on the patio, my vision traveling through the back yard, through the dark, leafy screen offered by the birch trees, reaching the second floor window of the ramshackle house on the other side of the ivy-covered brick wall behind my cottage, the only window to be seen with a light at this hour, a light I've learned to take for granted for it's always burning through the night, a banal shade of bare light from a simple bulb, this perfectly square window through which I could see nothing but the upper corner space of a dim yellow wall meeting a dull yellow ceiling in a room where the light for who knows what reason through the long night is always left burning.

THIS MUCH

Leaving the office, briefcase in hand, going down the stairs at a brisk pace, out through the heavy glass doors into the bright summer afternoon, then on the street, joining the dispersing flock, loosening my tie, striding along, a colleague falling into step beside me. "What's up with you for the evening?" he asks, removing his jacket, tossing it over his shoulder while I mutter about taking it easy at home. "I am off for a swim. That's my routine in such great weather. See you tomorrow," he says, turning at the corner, going his way in the currents of pedestrians. My clothes ruffled by the balmy summer breeze, the radiance of the sun creating a spectacle among the beguiling clouds, I continue along to the bus stop, glancing up at the clock on the church steeple, a dazzling ray of sunlight striking the gold-plated face, the hands and numbers invisible in the reflected radiance.

ENNUI

Short of breath when I climb the stairs. Always someone to say, "You should get more exercise." My look of bewilderment, another someone asks, "Do you know where you're going?" Taking a walk with a friend, I come to an abrupt halt. "Why are you stopping?" the friend wants to know. "I'd like to tell you something," I reply. "It's possible to walk and talk," the friend insists. In waiting rooms, exploring the deeper layers of waiting. At home, stretched out in my armchair, "I'll go out later when it cools off." A cloud of reverie hovering above me, a question whispered by the very air, "You will die and leave what behind?" My somber red blood, always eavesdropping, answering, "Ennui, ennui, ennui."

WARDROBE

Due to the everyday garments scattered, piled on the bed, going to bed means the clothes heaped on top of the blanket, weighing me down, and if a friend dropped by during the course of the day, first noticing the clothes, he would turn to the wardrobe, wipe the dust off the full-length mirror to get a better look at himself, open the door, observe the bare wooden hangers, the bleak interior like a wardrobe without an owner, stick his head inside, peering to the right, to the left, and at the dark, farthest corner, the dismal view of the hangers culminating in the sight of the elegant three-piece black suit, for accompaniment a tie strung on a separate hanger, a pair of well-polished formal black shoes down below, the friend saying, "Yes, indeed, a man must be prepared."

APOLOGY

I step off the curb only to be hurled through the air by a monstrous impact, landing, broken and bloody, on the asphalt, onlookers gawking, others glancing back over their shoulder, life ebbing away, my eyes wide open yet everything motionless, a freeze-frame in a movie. That's what almost happened but the bus managed a lurching halt inches before running me down, the driver's horror-stricken face reflecting much the same horror as mine, big windshield between us, my arms raised uselessly to ward off the blow, the stupefaction connecting the driver and me going on and on, time coming to a halt. I jump back to the curb, the driver glaring at me, he has seen a demon. The bus underway, I'm grinning brainlessly, waiting for a passer-by to stop and confirm the miracle. I want to be shaking hands, interviewed, but these fellow citizens, all of whom have borne witness, hastening on, detouring around me, a few sternly wagging their heads. Trembling, I take out my phone, dial a familiar number, the friend answers. My voice, hysterically high-pitched, "I've just escaped being run down. You won't believe how close." Wild shrieking words, describing the close-call, the stunned face of the driver. "OK. You survived. You're alive. Anything else you want to say?" The memory of the last time we'd met, we had argued, I'd become insulting, surely he's expecting me to say I'm sorry, sorry, terribly sorry.

WHEELBARROW

A wheelbarrow, full of rubble, placed on the sidewalk a bit off to the side, and I remember the time my father first taught me how to handle a wheelbarrow. Working in our backyard, he had filled it with dirt and stone, and I couldn't imagine conveying the heaping wheelbarrow without it overturning. My father taught me how, a question first of distribution, then of posture and intention. Your arms hanging down by your sides, elbows relaxed, bend your knees, keeping a straight back. Take hold of the handles with a firm grip, lifting slightly, the weight balanced between you and the wheel, then lean forward just a bit, setting the wheelbarrow in motion with your first step, and keep going, the wheel doing the work. You never forget how to handle a wheelbarrow once you have learned how, nor can I forget the thrill of moving it, fully loaded, doing my job the day I helped my father. This wheelbarrow topped up with debris, I bet I can convey it down the street, a long, empty stretch into the hazy distance, take hold and walk off, guiding it all the way back, arriving at our old house, my father still working in the yard, proving to him I haven't forgotten his instructions.

GRACE

One afternoon, while sauntering about on Main Street, I encounter a young couple standing in the middle of the sidewalk, pouring over a map, both of them hapless and distraught, and immediately I'm engaged in setting them on the right path, assuring them that they have indeed made a wise decision to pay a visit to our fair city at this time of the year, their look of joy and contentment inspiring even more glittering words while I go about the business of pointing out on the map the sights worth seeing, gesturing grandly, indicating well-known landmarks easily perceived around us. The gratitude flowing out of them helps me to realize how graciously I'm behaving, how cultivated and kind I truly am, motivating me to offer even further encouragement, walking with them part of the way and, before going on without me at their side, they praise my kindness which has served to remove the doubts they had been having. Bidding farewell, I allow my hands to touch each of them, just a light touch on his shoulder, on her arm, a healing touch actually. My glance falls on a homeless guy with straggly hair and the usual unwashed raggedy clothes sitting cross-legged under a tree on the corner, and he's got this beatific wide-eyed look focused on me, a radiant broken-toothed smile. I dig into my pocket for some small change to drop into the cup in front of him and instead take out my wallet, remove a fiver, which I hold out with the gentlemanly conviction of doing the right thing. Receiving my offering, the palms of his hands come together while he bows courteously, saying in a soft, enlightened voice, "The greatest wisdom is the wisdom of kindness. Help others." A divine gentleness flowing between us, like I'm barefooted, clad in a long robe, swaying with blessed, soundless laughter, intensely gleeful vibrations taking me over completely, shaking me free of all worldly cares. And now, with holiness coursing through my veins, I walk about, coming across two men standing in the middle of the sidewalk engaged in an argument about who did what to insult the other, their angry squawking beating the air, and it's easy enough to just bump into them thereby getting their attention, breaking their bitter, complaining rhythm, humbly apologizing for my carelessness while at the same time allowing my hands to drift into casual, tender contact, resting easily on their shoulders, giving each of them a pat on the back, transmitting divine kindness, pure goodness in my eyes. Soon they are offering charming smiles, uttering disarming words, placing their arms around each other so that we do achieve a brief unbroken circle of benevolence in the middle of the sidewalk, their faces lighting up.

Bowing, moving on, glancing behind to see them staring worshipfully after me, waving exuberantly, I raise my arms in blessing, this spreading of goodwill just another day's work, going to and fro, taking care of business.

PHOTO PLAY

Looking at the photo I took of the unmade bed after we had made love the last time, an aura of contemplation surrounding her, "It's all here," she says in a soft, faraway voice, "the sunlight on the unmade bed, the subtle play of shadows among the tangled covers. You can feel the breeze in the curtains. The breeze seems to come from an empty world outside the room, the delicate light creating the sense that the walls encroach and vanish simultaneously, the overall atmosphere one of presence and absence, of the lovers who've had an ecstatic night in this bed, They are here and not here. You can feel how they abandoned themselves, the tangled sheets and blankets, the contours of their bodies, their dance remains although they are gone. I know exactly how you took it. After I left you lay in bed, drifting off into a meditative state of bliss. You feel my presence. You feel my absence. You are in an in-between state, a twilight zone of desire. The room is haunted by what was, what is, what will be, and what at some time in the future won't be any longer. You get the camera. You wait for the perfect moment. And then you know, you just know." Then she says, "Something's happening. Can you feel it? Can you feel what's happening?" She takes my hand, her breathing soft, steady, a deep calm settling upon her. She's intensely alert, eyes flitting about, searching out what she senses. I'm caught in her intensity, her vision, and my senses lift me outside my usual self, the room possessing a transcendent gleaming quality. "Get the camera," she says, "and we'll just watch what's happening to time right now in this room."

HOLIDAY

I grow weary of the clear blue sea, the pure white beaches, the hypnotic palm trees, the mindless lying about in the sun, the glowing skimpily-clad suntanned bodies, and one morning, after struggling with the waves, managing to float on my back, staring at the dazzling sky, the strong swimmers stroking on by, heading for the horizon, after strolling aimlessly down the beach, trying to get the right holiday promenading on the beach posture, all I feel is sluggish and aimless, and after failing even at reclining in the sun, constantly sitting up, looking around to get some hints about how to be perfectly poised while reading or oiling my body, I banish myself, heading off, in a trance from too much sun, away from beach and hotel. Dazed, carried along by ubiquitous calypso music, I turn into a narrow unpaved street, little more than an alleyway where local stragglers wander about, in and out of rum shops, oblivious to my presence, a tourist in T-shirt and bathing-suit, along with the scraggly dogs and the one skeletal donkey with nowhere to go and all the time in the world to get there. I walk by a nondescript shop, and a large dark man wearing simple khaki clothes calls out to me, his voice kind and inviting, his gold-toothed smile full of charm and goodwill, assuring me that he has exact-ly what I need. Entering, I see a wide full-length mirror, and a black linen suit hanging on the wall, the man suggesting that I try on the suit, graciously assisting me, the suit a perfect fit, and he provides the appropriate shirt, modest tie, a dis-crete panama hat, along with the right shoes. Money not an issue, just pay later, I return to the hotel, to the beach, strutting about in my new outfit, set part from the hedonism of the holiday makers, their gaping bewilderment as they cast their hazy eyes in my direction. The intimacy of the sweat pouring off of me, the convic-tion of the man strong enough to stand alone, then heading on back to settle my bill, wondering what else the kind man might have to offer me, standing in the doorway, watching him busily at work. He's making something out of wood, saw-dust on the floor around him, tools within easy reach on his workbench. Glancing at me, then focusing again on the task at hand, he asks in a soothing voice, "Happy with your suit?" It's a coffin, he's making a coffin out of freshly hewn wood.

THE BRIDGE

I've got a bridge in my place, a slightly arched wooden bridge with railing, such as you're likely to find traversing a small garden pond, and since the bridge has been moved in I hardly bother with leaving my dwelling. The bridge takes up a fair amount of space in my less than spacious quarters, which isn't a problem because bridges exist to be walked across and crossing the bridge is what I spend a great deal of time doing, getting from desk to bookshelf, or fetching a drink from the fridge, or taking another look at myself in the mirror, or going to the window, looking out to see how the weather is shaping up, and numerous other impulses of daily indoor life that keep me in motion, and it isn't exactly going out of my way to cross the bridge. When I cross my bridge two loose boards clunk a bit, always the same dull sound of wood against wood, a rhythm that has become familiar and inviting, a stimulus that I miss when too many minutes have gone by without me hearing the noise, and I'm now always in my heavy boots which allow a stronger, more dramatic stride when crossing the rickety old bridge, often pausing in the middle, at the top of the arch, and from this vantage point surveying what lies around me, before me, behind me, no grand vistas, just the usual furnishings of life within these walls. Occasionally, with great exertion, I rearrange the bridge, shoulder placed against the railing, shoving with all my might until I manage to move the bridge, gouging out areas of the wooden floor, changing, in the interest of variety, the location points of crossing and arriving, but, given my living situation, the choices are limited, and the fact is that, regarding the crossing of the bridge, diversification isn't of the essence, crossing the bridge being simply crossing the bridge, not going across a raging current from one wild shore to the next, or finding myself suspended over a chasm praying that the bridge won't collapse. There are moments when, oblivious to the function of the bridge, I simply walk around, bypassing it altogether, these occasions leaving me with a bewildering feeling of having foregone an essential experience, but this forgetfulness now occurring much less often than when the bridge first became a part of my interior decoration.

OUT WEST

Waking up early to the raucous music of my creaky old bed in my shack just outside of town here in the looming quietude on the fringe of desert country, the sun already flashing its sabers at the window while I go about the daily business of slipping into my faded garments and these tired, aching old cowboy boots, all the while muttering to myself, "Seems like just yesterday," which gets me to chuckling. Stepping outside onto the ramshackle porch and looking out at the cactus and sagebrush, far off purple mountains, lizards scurrying about, one perched on the rocking chair, buzzards off aways, circling overhead, the silent ribbon of highway stretching into the hazy distance, tumbling tumbleweed as the wind picks up, shaking the old rickety structure. Then the screeching of the rusty apparatus while drawing water from the well, enough water to freshen up a bit, and not much else to do other than keeping out of the conquering sun, sitting on my porch, contemplating the giant cactus and the big old Joshua tree, the only green something as far as the eye can see, not to mention the occasional snake which is sure to appear if I just sit absolutely still and stare hard at all the holes under the rocks that comprise my front yard going on and on in all directions, boundary lines lost in the haze. I hear, drifting along on the breeze, the hoarse, plaintive feminine voice singing about whisky drinking, a broken heart, and those long nights when even the moon begins to cry, and there she is, the pale skinny lass in her skimpy red dress, holding her high heels, one shoe dangling from each outstretched hand, maintaining her balance, picking her way over the rocky ter-rain, though how she manages to stay pale with all that rambling about she does in the blazing eye of the sky I don't know, and my voice springs into action, saying as usual, "Can't believe you'd be walking around without shoes and all those dangerous snakes slithering around out there." And it's like she's still singing when she says, "I walk so lightly they hardly notice me and besides they'd hardly bother wasting their time with such slim pickings from a ghostly creature like me, and I might add that these are my dancing shoes and not your worldly desert wear," her words already so well-known to me that my lips move like I'm hum-ming along to a popular tune. "Been out dancing?" I ask, which gets the expected wild cackling laugh, and I wait one, two, three beats before adding, "Had yourself a wild night on the town, did you? That sinful place just a short distance over the next hill, Doomsday Saloon or whatever it's called?" By then she's sitting on the bottom step, the sweet, earthy fragrance of her sagebrush perfume emanating from her. She has already slipped on her shoes, blonde curls falling over her face, and she's tapping her feet rhythmically against a rock, and no redness whatsoever on her pale exposed skin so it must be that the sun just shifts its burning gaze to avoid her. "Seeing those buzzards got me worried about you," I say and she's giggling, having all the fun in the world. I call out, "Did you sashay across the dance floor with all those boys fighting over you? Come on now, 'fess up." And this gets her chortling even more as she says in that breathless voice of hers, "Guess I'm just set in my ways." Then adding, "With you a girl could sure die not just once but time and time again from pure rollicking laughter." The door to the shack opens and slams, and, just as I knew she would, she says, "Sure is nice to hear that sound of a door flapping in the wind, a door with nothing else to do but carry on like that, opening and closing and not a soul either coming or going." By then, shaded by the overhang of the porch roof, she's leaning back on her elbows, and the wind's picking up and she's watching the tumbling tumbleweed, and I'm rocking in my rocking chair and the old shack's shaking and rattling. I say, "If you'd like to share a meal I'd be glad to rustle us up some grub," which gets the anticipated outburst of a good belly laugh, the echoing, something otherworldly traveling through the barren surroundings. "Or would you rather that when the sun goes down I get my old bones a-moving and accompany you back over the hill where we could sit down to a proper dinner? You can count on me to get on out of there before the music starts for my dancing days are long gone." The last words we utter together in chorus and she's doubling over with hysterics by now and when her laughter dies down and the repartee trails off all's peaceful except for the wind and the tumbleweed and the door opening and slamming. Time does pass and when she's ready to slip away. I call after her, "One of these fine days I'll have to remember to get your name," and as usual, she says, "First I'll have to remember to commit it to memory." One high heel shoe held out in each hand, she's picking her way, singing the same old song, back into the desert from whence she came and I'm in my rocking-chair, thinking just another typical day in the hereafter, the sun setting, night coming on, coyotes beginning to howl, lost memories of days gone by when I used to tumble along with the tumbling tumbleweed.

LAST DANCE

Big band music from the thirties is being piped in at the home where my mother lives, nimble piano and elegant orchestration while I walk down the corridor to my mother's room. Fred Astaire comes on, singing "Dancing in the Dark" just as one of the pretty nurses appears who I greet with a few bars of song. She responds by opening her arms in a shall-we-dance gesture and right away I'm leading her in a few whirling steps only to be caught in the act by one of the ghostly, frail, gray-haired residents coming out of her room, barely managing to move along with her walker, exclaiming, "Fred Astaire and Ginger Rogers, Fred Astaire and Ginger Rogers." Her shrill excitement vibrates through the ward, my dancing cohort skipping off to tend to her other duties. The old ladies, dolled up in bright dresses and hairdos prim and perfect, emerge as if from thin air where they have been waiting out their memory loss, delicate, quivering, wide eyed with their wheelchairs, walkers, canes, calling out stridently, anxious to get it exactly right, "Fred and Ginger? Fred and Ginger?" But Ginger, already gone down the long corridor, being nowhere in sight, the dazzled audience settle on Fred. My mother, shuffling lightly through the flock, her skeletal frame a mere emanation from some source beyond her, eyes freshly alert, her words clear and well-reasoned, utters, "It's my son the dancer home from college for the weekend." A piercing tone interjects, "His college days are long past. Even I can see that," the speaker of truth a grand dame rocking back and forth in her wheelchair, her blazing eyes darting all around. "Dance son, dance!" my mother commands in a sparkling voice. Right on cue, my partner comes down the corridor, glimmering in her white uniform, and from the loudspeaker Fred's casting his spell with the yearning tones of "Let's Face the Music and Dance." The nurse and I are once more Fred and Ginger, deftly cavorting, her saying in her best, wry Ginger Rogers imitation, "Heck of a place for a girl to be swept off her feet." Then chirping words of clarity catch my ears, "He might be Fred but she's no Ginger because we know her." Still our dance routine continues until yet another wise observation stops us right in mid-step. "He doesn't have the right shoes. He doesn't even have the right shoes." The frolicking Florence Nightingale has to be moving along anyway, which she does with a gracious bow, and my mother, beaming at me, her face more halo than anything else, extends her fading, silken hand, saying, "Take my diamond ring. Buy yourself the right shoes. Make something of yourself. Come back for another dance when everything's just right."

MARCHING BAND

My last teaching assignment for the week, the Friday afternoon English class, reaches its end, the students filing out, voices and laughter down the corridor, down all the corridors on the campus come Friday afternoon, listlessness taking hold of me while I place my books and papers into my briefcase, an afternoon breeze wafting through the open window, rattling the blinds, sunlight casting its mild hopefulness over the rows of abandoned desks and chairs. In the vacant stillness, I can hear the echo of my own insistent voice, caught up in the repetition of days and classes, resounding back at me from the four bare walls, intermingling with the heavy clatter of construction work outside the window, a new building in the making. In the lull of Friday afternoon, the mélange of noise becomes steadily louder, every contribution more distinct, the space enclosing each sound adding an ongoing resonance, gruff, hard-working voices calling out on the scaffolding, cement mixers growling away, steady hammering, blazing of horns, dogs barking, the spirited cries of students, girls' high-pitched tinkling laughter, a young man's voice shouts, "Hey, wait for me," and I envision the student hurrying across campus to meet his friends. An ambulance siren in the distance, my hearing tagging along behind the plaintive cry, and then I hear the first notes of the marching band. The drum cadence, the clash of cymbals sparkling in the breeze, the reassuring chords of the trombones, the call of the trumpets, the notes dimly reaching my hearing, my ears anxious to catch the tune, my body wanting to join the ranks in all its splendor and glory, the music coming closer and closer, the dependable sound of the tubas. The everyday noise gets softer, fading into the background, finding their place in the rhythm of the marching band. I pack up my books and papers, shut my briefcase, slip on my jacket, the melody of the marching band a decorative frill to all that's happening. Picturing the musicians marching in step, their bright uniforms and shining epaulettes, proud sashes and plumage, the drum majorettes, their sleek high stepping legs in short skirts, glimmering batons like fairy-tale magic, I'm going down the steps, and passing a colleague, who tries to detain me with a question, I increase my pace, exclaiming, "There's a marching band!" I hit the streets, striding along. The marching band is approaching, and the people coming toward me are all foolishly going the wrong way. I should tell them to turn around and walk in the direction of the marching band, and the people in front of me are all walking too slowly. I should call out to them to hasten their pace. Surely they do not want to miss the marching band!

It's easy enough to stride past all of them because my strides are getting wider and wider, my smile getting ever brighter, choked up from the joy of knowing that at any moment the marching band will blaze into my vision, right around the next corner, or the next, or perhaps the marching band is now marking time somewhere just up ahead.

RED DRESS

She's wearing her red dress, a long, loose-flowing garment, and I linger behind for the pleasure of watching her stroll ahead, her lithe, bright, graceful form, the dark pines, sunlight on the water visible through the trees, the lacy hem of her dress caressing the ferns on the forest floor. She turns around to face me, waiting for us to continue side by side past the towering trees and dense undergrowth to our soft grassy secluded area on the river bank. This afternoon it's quiet on the river, coolness in the air, no playful voices calling out, the sound of hammering on the other shore, the summer camp being boarded up. No boats this afternoon, no swimmers, the wide, glimmering river looking somehow abandoned. A gust of wind catches us full in the face, rustling the trees. I lie down, figuring she'll take her place beside me, but she wants us to go for a final swim. I tell her it's too cool for that, let's just lie together by the riverside, and in one sudden motion she's on her feet, raising the dress off over her head, hanging the red dress on a branch, gone into the water, the red dress in the wind.

BEYOND

I'm supposed to sign and date the form and hand it back to the young nurse who has come this evening to administer the injection which will help propel me back to the realm of the survivors. She's standing in front of me, her posture stating, "Can't you just sign it so I can be on my way?" But I want to talk about my feverish delirium, though she's already said she's not able to help me with that, not having been my nurse at the hospital. I ask if there isn't someone whose job it is to sit at the bedside of delirious patients, taking down their ravings in shorthand. She says nurses don't learn shorthand. She's shuffling and fidgeting, emitting deep languishing breaths, scratching her arms, staring at the spider webs in the corners of the ceiling. I pick up the pen, intending to finally get it over with, but instead mention the very first time in my life, way back in my boyhood, when I'd heard the word delirious and how I knew right off from the solemn, lyrical, mysterious resonance of the word, that delirious was something I'd one day have to be, and when the doctor at the hospital confirmed that I had indeed been delirious, I knew the warm glow of success which comes with achieving a long sought after dream. The young nurse utters not a word of encouragement, so, scrawling my signature, I hand her the form. After examining it, she says in a desperate tone, "You must enter the place and date on the line next to your signature." I'm about to do as I am bidden, but seeing the empty line next to my signature, a space in eternity waiting for the officialdom of place and date, it feels like a death warrant, my eyes preoccupied with the vision of the pen falling from my hand, me keeling over onto the floor, babbling away, delirious, at last delirious once again.

THE HERMIT AND THE GUITAR

Just one more social obligation, a farewell party that friends have thrown together, a send-off that will last through the night and at dawn I'll be setting out directly for the forest to begin my new life as a hermit. Wearing my woollen hermit's robe, slipping into my sandals, picking up my wooden staff, lantern, and hermit's pack, pausing to take a last glance at this dwelling that has provided shelter during my final years among the masses, worldly goods left behind, on impulse, figuring that one of the partygoers will have use for it, I also take along the old guitar that has been gathering cobwebs in the corner these many years, learning to play the guitar being one of the numerous projects I never completed during my days of quiet desperation. By the time I arrive, the party's in full-swing. I set down my pack, staff, lantern, and guitar, the host proclaiming that the guest of honor has at last appeared, the revellers swarming around me, some admiring my hermit's garment, others finding it a bit too long, the cut not so flattering, some tugging childishly at my beard and long, unkempt hair, remarking that I already have that dour look of a recluse, cameras flashing, photos of me with staff and lantern, with cowl raised and cowl lowered, group photo with hermit, and of course the ongoing chatter and puerile questions regarding the living conditions of a hermit, encouraging pats on the back, someone asking if visits would be permitted, someone else responding that you don't visit a hermit because a hermit is a hermit. Holding up the guitar, I ask, "Who'd like a guitar?" A hushed moment ensues. And then, "I didn't know you played the guitar." I try to explain that because it's my guitar that doesn't mean I can play the guitar, but no one's listening, pronouncements following in quick succession, "I knew you were lonely but I didn't know you played the guitar, I knew you were a loser with women but I didn't know you played the guitar, I knew you were a lost soul but I didn't know you played the guitar, I knew you were socially inept but I didn't know you played the guitar, I knew you were a good-for-nothing but I didn't know you played the guitar." And all the while I'm being trundled along by the throng, voices rising with the demand, "Give us a song, give us a song." I'm installed in a chair in the center of the living room. "Come on hermit, we want music, we want music." I keep protesting, saying I can't play the guitar, but the chorus of rhythmic chanting drowns me out. "I knew you were a weirdo but I didn't know you played the guitar, I knew you were a wallflower but I didn't know you played the guitar, I knew you had an inferiority complex but I didn't know… etc. etc." And carried along by the insistent voices, I begin to strum the out of tune dust covered cob-webbed guitar, strumming without any notion of how to even strum a guitar, strumming like a rock 'n roll star gone mad, bellowing along with the group, "I knew you were a jerk but I didn't know you played the guitar. I knew you had fallen by the wayside but I didn't know you played the guitar." I'm in a frenzy, strumming, pounding on the guitar, howling, and soon I'm on my feet, doing an Elvis imitation, my hermit's robe swirling around me, my legs getting entangled in the material, my head tossing from side to side, hair and beard flying around like sparks, my friends, one at a time, adding their favorite line. "I knew you wasted your life but I didn't know you played the guitar, I knew you watched a lot of soap operas on TV but I didn't know you played the guitar, I knew you read a lot of philosophy but I didn't know you played the guitar. I knew you went to the movies alone on Saturday nights but I didn't know you played the guitar, I knew you never cooked a decent meal but I didn't know you played the guitar." There's no stopping us and the night passes, the first glimmer of dawn finding us still going strong, our voices painfully hoarse, until it's time for me to be on my way. My friends walk me to the door where I pick up my staff, my lantern, my pack, and step out into the breaking of a new day, strolling off down the road, looking back for the last time at those gathered together on the doorstep, waving goodbye. I make my way to the forest, the old guitar left behind.

AUTUMN AT THE LAKE

We're enjoying the colorful autumn, the freshly melancholic crimson season, the charming grayness of the afternoon clouds, the shiver of autumn awakening the feverish sensation of the dark root in the body. We idle along the carpet of leaves around the lake, a pensive mist hovering above the glossy waters, and a bird, which we instantly label the autumn bird, chirps a sad melody. A deer, with gently quivering strides, steals through the afternoon, down to the water's edge, causing us to stand perfectly still, caught up in the suspense, leaves, inflamed by the colors of autumn, spinning in the crisp air around us. We're standing so magically still we hardly notice that the deer has gone and we continue to stand like statues while the wind sweeps the leafy golden earth. Then we promenade by the dark autumnal body of water while the twilight comes on. Through the big picture window in our bungalow, lying in bed we have a view of the autumnal darkness, and when I awake, startled to find myself alone, in the dim light I see you standing by the window, observing the stealth of the autumn dawn.

CURTAINS

The curtains, they don't hang right. They don't hang straight. There's certainly something out of kilter in the fall of material from ceiling to floor, a basic unevenness about these curtains, although from outside you don't notice. I went outside and looked and from outside everything's fine, like finally someone cares enough about living here to get curtains and hence that desolate look of big, naked glass window is now a thing of the past. But from inside the apartment, when you're just sitting here and looking with critical eyes directly at the curtains, it's obvious they don't hang right. Perhaps it has to do with the cheapness of the fabric. I didn't invest too heavily, and then I took the material to the seamstress right round the corner and a few days later I picked up the curtains and when I got home I hung the curtains, but they obviously don't look right. Something is off, yet I suppose the long dark nights will be a bit better now with the curtains. Then a friend comes in and suggests that I take them back, not the long dark nights because how could I possibly take those back, pack up my long dark nights in a cardboard box, drive out to the all-night department store and say, "Hi, remember me? I came in here a few nights ago about this time and I bought this box of long dark nights and, well, now I'm bringing them back because they're just not what I had in mind." But the curtains, this friend can see that the fault is in the sewing and it's only right and fair that the seamstress should correct her mistakes. This friend, he wants to right a wrong, and because there's nobody weeping behind the curtains, nobody seeking refuge, nobody ready to jump out and say what's the big idea, he has all the time in the world to make his case, all the time in the world.

SONGS

This morning I just can't stay seated with my briefcase on my lap, daily newspaper shielding me from all my fellow commuters on the commuter express, so I get to my feet, carried along by the rhythm of the speeding non-stop train, my voice shrieking with the pure tormenting rage of heartbreak, "Well, since my baby left me/Well, I found a new place to dwell/Well, it's down at the end of Lonely Street/At Heartbreak hotel". Hips swiveling, "Ill be so lonely baby/Well I'm so lonely/I'll be so lonely, I could die". Getting that kind of mad hiccupping pure Elvis cry, I'm strumming my briefcase, rocking in the aisle, tie flapping,   buttons popping open, shirt out of my pants by now, jacket slipping off my shoulder, my fellow passengers glancing up from their newspapers, taking a brief look at me, smiling a subtly tolerant understanding smile. The train's in the station, passengers automatically rising, me fixing my clothes, tie properly arranged. I emerge from the station to find Louis Armstrong waiting for me, gleaming trumpet in hand, fingers itching to get started, offering his benevolent kind-uncle smile, falling into step beside me, asking in that mischievous throaty drawl with wide magnanimous smile and divinely wrinkled countenance, "What will it be this morning?" Right away I burst into song, not too loud, just between me and Louis, "I've seen skies of blue/Clouds of white/Bright blessed days/Dark sacred nights", that deep, slow, hoarse, drawn-out enunciation that I've picked up from him, having all the time in the world to get the words out because I'm feeling what there is to feel, "And I say to myself what a wonderful world." Louis, taking it easy on trumpet, providing the melody line, letting me go at it my way, and I'm not making a fuss so that the pedestrians feel threatened and have to detour around me and Louis, but letting the lyrics flow from the deep old man river that Louis' presence offers. "I see friends shaking hands/Saying how do you do/They're really saying I love you ..." And when I arrive at the office, Louis is already gone into thin air, leaving me alone to enter the building, the whole day ahead of me.

IN THIS

Driving up north in the snowstorm, one detour after another, slipping and sliding along through the blizzard, the small towns in their snug locations, past the houses securely snowed in, no one out and about, neither children nor snowmen, night coming on, a world of windblown whiteness lit by pale streetlights, for accompaniment the tinkling sound of the tire chains along with the steady rhythm of the windshield wipers, a metronome of urgency while I drive along enclosed like an alien in my capsule, moving slowly through a landscape in which only arrival counts, the car rocking and lurching through mounds upon mounds of endless snow. I park in a snow bank, exit into the glacial wind, the driven snow, trudging across the trackless arctic expanse to the front door. I stomp in, a holy stillness in the house, flickering shadows and candlelight, the steady roaring of wind and snow, the group, sitting cozily by the fireplace, turning their hazy faces in my direction, a few extra beats before Kay, putting aside the blanket, rises dreamily from her armchair, standing in place like she's lost all sense of motion, asking in a sleepy, faraway voice, "How did you ever make it up from the city in this?" A woman's voice joins in, startled into wakefulness, "I can't believe he managed to drive up from the city in this!" Dazed after the hours of steadfast journeying, the vision of snow everywhere, I can only glance from one somnolent countenance to the next. "How did you make it up from the city in this?" The news spreading through the house, more and more drowsy beings keep appearing, ghost-like, out of the communal recesses of darkness hidden away in the old mansion, and Kay, dazzled, taking small steps in my direction, keeps repeating, "Can you believe he drove all the way up from the city in this?" A dazed looking fellow, absorbed in tugging at his beard, strolls in, pointing at me, gawking, making as if to fall over backward. "Am I hearing right? Unbelievable." Snow piling up more and ever more at the windows, "But we're snowbound!" a man exclaims, staring into the fire, giving the matter careful thought. Kay, her accustomed smile beginning to take shape, her arms reaching out, while the wind roars, snow falls, and the house shakes.

TARZAN

Enough of this daily life, the slings and arrows of one damn defeat after another, I'm out the door, fleeing my desk, dashing like mad in the hot sun, leaping the spiked iron fence, streaking wildly into the jungle, for nothing can stop me from sacrificing myself to the lions down by the river, and if the lions are busy elsewhere then the rapids, the elephants, the tigers, the gorillas, a cliff I can tumble over. Enough, I scream, careening through the dense undergrowth, birds and lesser animals scampering out of my frenzied path. The roar of a lion nearby, the end is upon me! Then, "AAHAAAA," the high-pitched achingly human call of a man without words, the lonely melody vibrating through my heart, a counterpoint to the savage growling of the lion, man alone among the beasts, here he comes, swinging through the trees, sweeping me up with the greatest of ease. I'm snatched from the jaws of certain death, the golden beast left gaping in disappointment, the jungle whirling by, ease of flight, strength and purpose, I swoon when he tosses me over his shoulder. Now he is setting me down right where I started from, his gleaming physique, his faithful eyes dispelling all fear. A kind of squinting, puzzled, irate expression that must mean, "Don't pull any of this weird rushing to your death stuff again, Ok?" His hands pushing, pushing the air, gesturing me to stay right where I am, it's a jungle out there. Work to do. No time to waste, "AAHAAAA," the melodious pain of it all.

PURPOSE

Sitting in a café, savoring a glass of wine, peaceful chatter flourishing all around me, then a man is standing at my table, engaged in trying to sell a leather jacket. His English being almost incomprehensible, I understand he needs money to get somewhere in the far-off mountains, and the jacket is of genuine leather. A hushed silence ensues, all the faces now turned toward me. "Well, my good chap, a genuine leather jacket, is it? Would you mind if I tried it on before making my final decision?" The waitress comes by, saying she'd be glad to assist, taking the leather jacket from the foreign gentleman, who has assumed the pose of deep dignity coupled with humility and eternal patience. The waitress holds the jacket for me to put on. "An absolutely perfect fit, the living image of elegance and composure," someone in the audience calls out, and they all nod in agreement, muttering their approval. The waitress says, "Let's give them both a big hand." Applause thunders through the café while I reach into my pocket, remove my wallet, graciously counting out in crisp new currency the asked for sum to pay the gentleman from the far off mountains while he exclaims in his broken English that his yearning for home will soon be fulfilled. He and I bow together to the audience before he departs, backing away toward the door, his gold-toothed smile shining in the air. The faces turning away, engaging once more in conversation, the waitress continuing with waiting on tables, I notice that my new leather jacket is actually a bit tight in the shoulders. Seated once again in my now familiar spot, I observe the grace of the waitress, feel myself soothed by the murmur of nearby voices, and weep quietly with the joy of having today accomplished a worthy task.

WIND CHIMES

On the bookshelf by my bed, a photo of my mother's grave, with me sitting on the grass under the nearby tree, the grave marker with her name, dates of birth and death, including an engraving of a saying my mother liked, that the race is not to the swift but to he who endures to the end. Just before I sat down on the grass, I'd hung wind chimes in the tree but they do not appear in the photo because we wanted to photograph the grave marker. The chimes sounded in the wind while I waited for the picture to be taken, imagining how my mother's face would have lit up if she'd been there to hear the gentle harmonious sounds. On my bookshelf, another photo of my mother, in her garden, her delighted expression, surely she's hearing wind chimes, and I'll be getting my very own, hanging them outside my bedroom window, hearing the gentle knell at night, glancing at the photos just before shutting out the light.

THE BREEZE

A balmy breeze wafts through the open door of the cafe, a delicious breeze full of goodwill, and right away my yawning, stretching, sighing begins, this breeze having been sent my way to restore a forgotten need, my mouth opening in engulfing yawns. A woman comes in and sits at a table across from mine, and she too is yawning, sighing, stretching, the benign breeze enveloping us both while we surrender to one irrepressible yawn after another. Then a man is standing at her table. He has obviously hurried to get here to be with her. She gives him a brief greeting and continues with her sighing, stretching, yawning while his eyes dart from her to me and back again, the young woman and I caught in the angelic spell of the breeze. He sits down next to her, his presence breaking the spell for a moment as they converse, but then the breeze wafts even stronger and it all starts up once more. He puts his arms around her to contain her, but she moves away, surrendering to the breeze. I would like to let him know it's simply the balm of the breeze all around us, but I'm unable to stop myself from yawning, sighing, stretching, and because he has placed himself beyond the influence of the balmy breeze wafting its benevolence through the café, and because he appears troubled by what's happening, I get up, fumbling in my pockets for some small change to place on the table before going out once again into the hot afternoon.

HAPPY MAN

I'm getting out of bed when I hear a voice. "You're a happy man." It's my own voice, escaping without permission, the voice adding, "You've made it." "Ok, if you say so," I answer, figuring I'll play along, joining the fun and games. Happiness is something that has always belonged to other people so I sit on the edge of the bed, waiting for the daily despondency to set in, dredging up a series of past failures to help it along. What follows is a roar of laughter, echoing down the gloomy byways of my usual repertoire of memories, and the laughter's all mine in the here and now. I must be out of touch with reality this morning so to return to normal I look in the mirror, pointing out my lack of muscles, my having neither good looks nor good fortune. "Who cares!" This time it's me exclaiming, singing out, "I've got plenty of nothing and nothing's plenty for me." Lines to a popular song adding a touch of glory to the situation, I then make my morning tea, slump in my usual chair, enjoying the view from up here nicely framed in the glass door to the balcony, fresh morning light, clear blue sky, the new day coming at me, riding the familiar wave of roof tops, without complaint.

PALS

After midnight, I'm getting ready for bed when the phone rings, my chum from the good old days, whose life has been on the skids these last years, calling, which he does occasionally in the late hours when melancholic nostalgia takes hold of him, from some dismal dive in the section of town known for its sleazy nightlife, some joint with mawkish songs on the jukebox, and I can just envision him, my debauched old crony, staggering drunk by now, phone in one hand, drink in the other, sentimental tears streaming down his decadently, handsome face, standing at the jukebox, singing along in a maudlin voice, an aged barfly floozy in low-cut dress hanging onto him. I can hear Sinatra's voice in the background singing "My Way" and can't help but gasp mockingly at my pal's audacity, for, instead of a normal greeting like "Hello dear friend, hope I'm not disturbing you at this late hour. I'm sitting in a lonely bar remembering the good old days and on impulse gave you a call," instead of some kind of expected salutation of a similar nature, in a deep baritone he sings along into the phone, "Regrets I have a few/ but then again too few to mention/ I did what I had to do/ and saw it through without exception", and I'm thinking if anybody should have regrets surely he should, for he has definitely wasted his days on earth, falling into a life of roguish dissipation, deception and shady dealings that has led naturally to his being an outcast, alone and lonely. He let's this self-flaunting panegyric of a song play in my ear before speaking in that deep, mellow sorrowfully charming voice of his, how about joining your eternal comrade for a late night drink and let's stand shoulder to shoulder once more against the passage of years? I can just see him, his deep watery disconsolate eyes tempting you to offer consolation, his villainously attractive features, black curly hair that must be mostly gray by now, the epitome of the dissolute romantic, looking debonair in a worn-out suit that had been once stylish, and I know all he wants is for me to go and keep him company at the desolate bar, drinking all night, recalling our glory days, and then walking out arm in arm, singing on the way home, dawn breaking over the rooftops. I tell him to give me a call some other time, and let's arrange in advance to meet for dinner, for I have to be at the office early in the morning, which of course leads to him turning on the mournful charm even more, wanting to get me feeling guilty about neglecting him, my soul mate, me managing to silence his persistent plea by politely hanging up the phone. But I can't sleep, his haunting voice, the swirl of memories, the bright lights and big city we once knew together, the stream of women through our bachelor pads, the tender traps we learned to weave with charm, promises, and perseverance, our ongoing intoxicated discussion about the meaning of it all, and now my old ally calling out for me! What he needs is some-one to help him get back on track, to show the way to a decent life, provide an opportunity, and moved along by the determination that comes when a man is doing what he knows he must do, I am soon dressed and out the door, invigorated, hastening through the late-night streets, turning left, turning right, crossing the railroad tracks, a freight train chugging by, its lonesome whistle adding poign-ancy to the night. I head on into the neon-lit lowlife area, passing cheap hotels, avoiding the streetwalkers wanting to ensnare a last customer for the night, out of breath by now, my mind rehearsing the words I will speak to my comrade-in-arms. I burst into his usual joint, and there he is, standing at the bar next to a woman who must have been a blonde bombshell in a previous life, a few other hopeless cohorts scattered randomly about, each one staring into their glass, the morbidly dark, squalid atmosphere, and Sinatra's voice with full orchestra, includ-ing harp strings, blaring through the place like a hymn, singing about standing tall and taking the blows and doing it my way, and my pal and his voluptuous companion joining in, raising their voices with great enthusiastic harmonious celebration, Jack swaying with a drink in one hand, the other arm raised victori-ously, the blonde throwing her head back and pelting out the tune while she clings to my confidante from the distant past. Anxious and in a hurry because I do have to get up in the morning and face another day at the office, I can see that my friend, though grayer and worn-out from his life of dissipation, still hasn't com-pletely lost his famous force of personality, and it takes a moment for him to recognize that I, the bosom friend he's been calling randomly over the years, am here in the flesh. Wanting to speak my piece and be done with it, get on out of there, afraid of succumbing to his allure and staying all night, I embrace him, whispering that I've come to offer my help because I know he's fallen on hard times, but he keeps interrupting me, his twinkling, mischievous eyes making it hard to continue, and his consort seems to be taking a liking to me, and the bartender has made his way towards us and wants know what I'd like to drink. My voice gets louder and louder, intending to drown out his skillfully enchanting voice constantly intruding into mine, saying, "Old pal, I think of you everyday. What times we used to have! Let me get you a drink, let me introduce you to ..."

and the woman is taking my hand and beaming at me, and I'm saying I didn't come here to drink and reminisce. It's not too late. I am willing to help pull you out of the lower depths you've fallen into. He's muttering, "Very kind of you but let's have a drink together once more for the good times." And I'm saying I wish I could sit here and drink with you through the night like we used to do in the bygone era but to be honest it's already way past my bedtime. I embrace him, emotion surging up in me. "Don't call again until you're ready to let me help you get back on the track of a decent life, starting with dinner at my place during which we will lay out the groundwork for your redemption." And I make for the door, the woman saying in my wake "I didn't understand a damn word that guy uttered," and my old amigo joining in, saying in a well-modulated tone, "Neither did I, honey, neither did I."